MIGUELITO

LEAVES

CUBA

FOR

AMERICA

A True Story

By Michael Ruiz, Jr.

Illustrated By: Dwight Nacaytuna

Copyright © 2015 by Michael Ruiz, Jr. 703551
Library of Congress Control Number: 2015916294

ISBN: Softcover   978-1-5035-3484-1
         EBook   978-1-5035-3485-8

Print information available on the last page

Rev. date: 11/30/2015

To order additional copies of this book, contact:
Xlibris
1-888-795-4274
www.Xlibris.com
Orders@Xlibris.com

About The Author

Michael Ruiz escaped Communist Cuba as eight year old boy. With his mother and father, he left on a cargo boat which departed for Africa. From Havana, Cuba, to Morocco, Africa, then to Portugal, and finally to New York City, America, it was a unique and incredible adventure for a little boy. Mike Ruiz went on to Brooklyn to join relatives, then on to enjoy American freedom. After college, he would become a teacher of English, Spanish, and Italian, as well as a tennis coach. He married and had two wonderful children, Michelle and Stephen. After 30 years, Mike Ruiz is still teaching at Manhasset Middle School and High School on Long Island, New York. With a great passion, he loves la familia, his two children—whom he calls the brilliant light of his life—his granddaughter Hayden, wife Lida, father Miguel, wife Sandra, and brother Miguel Alejandro.

For mi bella madre, Isela, who taught me to be strong, that there is nothing more significant than la familia, and to never forget Cuba. Te quiero mucho [I love you] Mami.

And for another beautiful girl—Hayden Mary, my granddaughter, whose wonderful character, intelligence and smile remind me of her great grandmother Isela.

Acknowledgements

Gracias to my father, my best friend, who has always been there for me. To Sandra and my dear brother Miguel Alejandro—God bless you for your benevolence and love.

Mijos, my daughter Michelle and son Stephen Michael, you will always be the brilliant light of my life—with you, I will never be in darkness. A father is nothing without his kids and grandkids. Daniel, you are my second son. I love ya'll so very much.

To my wife Lida—at times when no one else seems to be around, you are by my side. Gracias—te quiero.

Mis primos, tíos and true amigos in NY, Florida, Puerto Rico and Cuba—let us embrace familia. I am blessed to have you in my life.

To my Manhasset Middle School and High School students of italiano and español, my tennis players, the members of the Rachel's Challenge Club, grazie/gracias for making every day of my life truly challenging, very meaningful and so enjoyable! Your daily, kind gestures and words, cards and tri-colored cupcakes for my birthday, mean the world to me, and I will always be grateful to you for your respect and love. I love you guys—BLR ["Be Like Rachel"] and Carpe diem for life!

To my friends at X-Libris: Mike Stewart, Jay Fairchild, artist Dwight Nacaytuna, Rey Santos and all else who helped me to finally publish this memoir—muchas gracias.

Havana, Cuba

Miguelito* [Michael, Mikey] Ruiz Asenjo was born in Havana, Cuba, in the late 1950's, just sixty miles from "la Florida", America. His Mamá* Isela was a housewife and his Papá*[Dad] Miguel drove a cigar truck for a company named "Partagas". Cuban cigars are the best and most expensive in the world. Although they didn't have a great deal, they were very happy. Every night when Papi came to el apartamento* [apartment], Mami cooked a delicious meal like arroz con pollo,* [rice with chicken], la ensalada* [salad], and maybe papas* [potatoes]. Miguelito was so happy to see his Papi come home from work, as Papi would kiss Mami and hug his son who would run quickly and spring into Papi's outstretched open arms. It was a joyous time in Cuba.

La escuela *[school]* y la familia *[family]*

When he was five, Miguelito would go to la escuela* *[school]* by bus. It was a very good school where he learned mucho* *[much]* and had plenty of tarea* *[homework]*. He liked school and his padres* *[parents]* explained to him how very important la educación* *[education]* was in Cuba. They also explained to him that Cuba had one of the highest "literacy" rates, [number of people who are able to read], in the world.

After school Miguelito and his Mama would walk to Tía* *[aunt]* Ofelia's casa *[house]*. It was a very nice brick home of two stories. There he would play with Conchita, his prima* *[cousin]*. Conchita had dos* *[two]* hermanos* *[brothers]*: Kiko *[Roberto]* and Manolito *[Manny]*. Also Abuela* *[Grandmother]* Catuca *[Catalina]* lived with them.

Abuela Catuca was the matriarch of the familia* *[familia]*; she was the leader of the familia. As a single Mamá, she had raised six wonderful children: Lidia, Ofelia, Fernando, Eugenio, Isela and Manolito. Abuela would work hard at her job all day long in a hot factory, then at night she would sew emblems for policemen's uniforms to make a little extra money.

Abuela Catuca and Tía Ofelia had a big, beautiful, black German Sheppard, Sultán. Papi loved animales* *[animals]* so much, and when Papi visited, he would whistle in a special way and Sultán would start jumping and barking, almost jumping Tía Ofelia's black, wrought iron fence. It was so much fun being with la familia* *[family]* every day of his life on the bella* *[beautiful]* island of Cuba.

Monterrey, a new home

One day Miguelito saw Mami very upset. His Abuelo* *[Grandfather]* Miguel had passed away. Abuelo loved Miguelito, as he was named after him. Many Cuban boys were named after their Papi and grandpa. The little boy didn't understand, but Mami said that Abuelo had gone to Heaven with Dios *[God]*. Now they moved in with Abuela* *[Grandma]* María and Bisabuela* *[Great Grandma]* Amparo to Monterrey, a suburb about twenty minutes away from his apartment in Havana, la capital* *[capital],* to a very nice casa* *[home]* with a garden, a yard with a chicken house that housed chickens of bright rainbow colors like red, yellowish, brownish… and a busy rooster, who would often jump on the chickens. The boy guessed that the rooster wanted attention. Abuela Amparo would enter the chicken house in the morning and grab the chickens and feel for an egg that would soon be hatched. The Cubanito noticed that the poor chickens were not very happy to see Abuela enter the chicken coop every morning!

They had a dog named "Oso" *[bear],* but he was not very friendly—only to great-grandma. Oso was left by Tíos* *[Uncle and Aunt]* Juan and Tiá Nelly when they left Cuba for Puerto Rico. Tíos* Juan and Nelly didn't want to live in Cuba anymore, so they left with primos* *[cousins]* Juanito, Neni (Nelly) and Susy to Puerto Rico, another beautiful island where they speak español* *[Spanish].* There Alex and Roxana would be born and Tío Juan's business selling medicina* *[medicine]* to pharmacies would make him very successful. The very hard trabajo* *[work]* and success of the tres tíos* *[three uncles]* would serve as a model for los primitos* *[little cousins]* for the rest of their lives.

El niño* *[the boy]* had a new home, new school, and even chickens and a gallo bravo* *[rooster].* He had also made friends with Lilianita and he felt that he had "fallen in love" with her. Miguelito walked to school with Liliana and her hermana* *[sister]* Olguita. After school Mami always made el niño* *[boy]* slices of Cuban pan* *[bread]* toasted on the oven and then buttered with love. Mami called them "cochinitos," *[little pigs].* Now dinner was with Abuelas María, Amparo, Mami y* *[and]* Papi, Mochito and Oso, los perros* *[dogs].*

A New "Presidente"* [President] for Cuba

Something happened when Miguelito was about cinco* [five]. He heard Mami and Papi and la familia talking about a man named "Castro". He was the Presidente* [President] of Cuba. They seemed afraid, not happy of this change. Now Mami and Abuela had a booklet called "la libreta"* [booklet]. It was used to buy food, but only a certain amount of food was allowed. La familia blamed "los rusos"* [the Russians] for this booklet. Miguel recalls that one night Papi was returning from a business trip to Isla de Pinos where he was trying to sell head bands for girls. There was one more small bistec* [steak] left and the little boy was still hungry, so Mami let him eat it because she did not expect Papi back. Yet a short while later Papi showed up and announced that he was starving. Miguelito, Mami and Abuela looked so sad and guilty as there was nothing to eat. Papi was not upset, but when he went to the fridge looking for eggs—there was nothing there but agua* [water]. The little boy would recall this painful experience for the rest of his life. Cubanos* [Cubans] did in fact go hungry. In la escuela* [school], the teachers talked about "Comunismo,"* [Communism], but Mami and Papi did not agree with that type of government. They said we should be "libre"* [free], like America!

los domingos: Sundays

Now every domingo* *[Sunday] at Tía* [aunt] Ofelia's,* the tíos* *[uncles]* "Papito" Manolo, Fernando, Luis and Papi, playing dominoes and drinking café espreso* *[expresso coffee]*, talked about Castro and the new rules, but Abuela Catuca urged them, "Cuidado!"* *[Careful!]*, keep quiet or they would get in big trouble. Las tías* *[aunts]* cooked ropa vieja* *["old clothing": shredded beef with tomato sauce]* and talked in la cocina* *[kitchen]*. Miguel played with los primos* *[cousins]* and even Ginita [Gina] and Asela came with los tíos* *[aunts and uncles]* Lidia and Jorge. Aunt Lidia had sky blue eyes-wow. Miguelito played much with Ginita, as they were closer in age. They played tag and "el Escondido"* *[hide and seek]* in Tía Ofelia's big house. Sultán chased them barking, but Papi would tell him, "Silencio!"* *[Be quiet!]*. La familia* *[family]* was so special, grande* *[big],* and it was the best día* *[day]* of the week! Little did he realize, the little cubanito *[Cuban boy]* would dearly miss this *familia* in America for the rest of his life.

A Very Scary Day

One day Mami came to school and took Miguel home in a terrible rush because Tío* *[Uncle]* Fernando had called her and told her to take him home immediately. Miguelito heard that there was something like a war going on. Mami told him that he had to hide under the bed to be more secure in case anything bad happened. They called it the next day the *"Bay of Pigs Invasion"*. He didn't understand it, but it was a group of Cuban-Americans from the USA trying to free Cuba from this new government called "Comunismo,"* *[Communism]*. Many Cuban-Americans from Miami did not succeed in the attack. It was very sad. They would never see their families again. The next day things seemed ok, but la familia* *[family]* was disappointed that Cuba was not libre* *[free]* again. Mami said not to worry about it—things would be fine. Isela--Mami had a special way of reassuring him and making el niño* *[the boy]* feel fine—secure and loved.

Shocking News

One day Miguelito came home after school and Papi was home. He did not go to work to drive the cigar truck. While Mami made him "cochinitos,"* *[little pigs]*, Italian bread with butter and café con leche* *[coffee with milk]*, the boy learned that Papi could no longer work because they were leaving beautiful Cuba to hopefully move to freedom in America—the United States! Miguelito did not know how to react. How could he leave his familia* *[family]*, amigos* *[friends]*, his casa* *[home]* with the chickens and a rooster? He knew no inglés!* *[English]*, so how could he even talk to the kids in America?! Mami and Papi reassured him that things would be fine-"Todo va a estar bien, Mijito."* *[Everything would be ok, my little son]*—Just concentrate on school and la tarea* *[homework]*.

Miguelito could no longer go to school!

Miguelito was overhearing strange stories of how neighbors were taking their families on motor boats and escaping to Florida, America. Yet this was dangerous, so Papi would not do this, as some made it to Florida while others were caught by the Cuban Coast Guard and jailed. One day Mami spoke to el niño* [the boy] and told him that he could no longer attend school. Miguelito was shocked and very saddened—how could he not go to school! He was just in 3rd grade, and he loved learning. The problema* [problem] was that in school they were teaching about "Comunismo,"* and Mami y Papi were very upset about this. They strongly believed in "democracia",* [democracy]—a free government like in America.

At la casa [home], Miguelito had to read many libros [books] that la familia had given him. His primo Pepito had left for Spain with his Abuela* Chucú [Carmen], and they left Miguel many books—very interesting. (Tía Chucú would leave for Spain and then to Florida, where she raised Pepe with great love and affection.) So Mami would read with him and encourage him to read every day. Yet he so missed school, his amigos* [friends], the tarea* [Homework] and walking to school with la bella* [beautiful] y simpática [nice], sweet Lilianita!

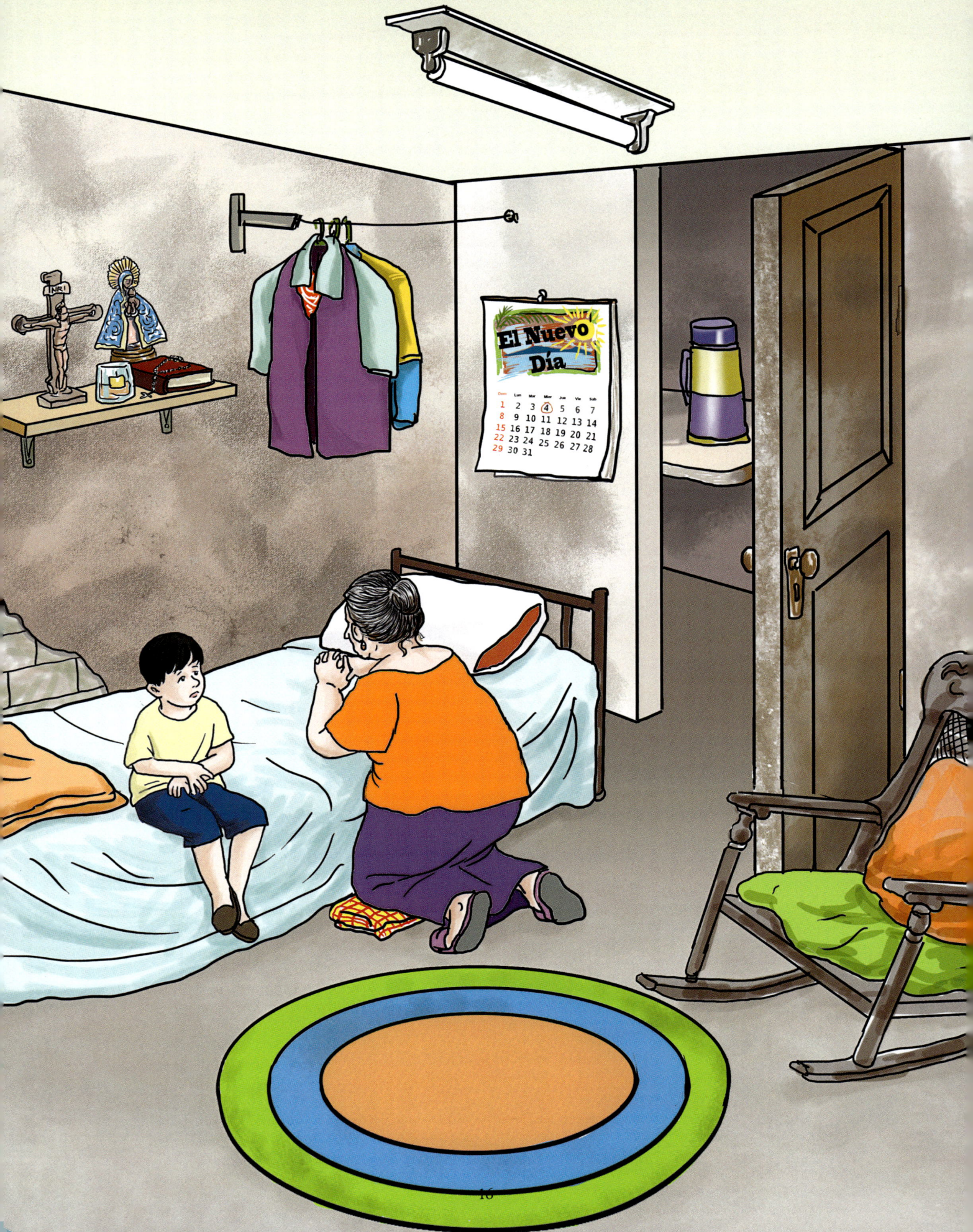

Evening Prayers with Abuela [Grandma] María

In Miguelito's new home in Monterrey there was no bedroom for him so he slept with Abuela María. The first night that he went to bed in the nice new home, he said, "Buenas noches" *[Good night]* to Mami and Papi, kissed and hugged them, then Mami put him to bed. Abuela María then entered the room, and as el niño went to say, "Buenas noches", Abuela knelt down by the side of the bed. She blessed herself, "In the name of el Padre, el Hijo, y el Espíritu Santo,"* *[Father, the Son, and the Holy Spirit]*, finishing by kissing her thumb and index finger. Abuelita* *[Grandmother]* then folded her hands and prayed to God. Miguelito did not know exactly what to do, so he watched his Abuela pray for a while. She then finished, blessed herself again, and went to bed. She kissed her nieto* *[grandson]* good night on his forehead, and told him to always thank God for all that we have, even though they had much less now, they still had much more than others who were starving in other parts of the world— "Always say 'gracias'* *[thank you]* Miguelito."

La Playa [beach] Santa María [St. Mary Beach]

Sometimes Papi would come home early from his job driving the cigar truck, and even Tío [Uncle] Luis would also come home early from the jewelry store and Papi would say to his son, "Vamos a la playa!"* [Let's go to the beach!] Miguelito was so excited as it was summer time and he loved the beach. So Papi, Tío Luis and el primo* [cousin] Luisito would get in Papi's blue Chevy and drive to the beautiful beach, la Playa* Santa María. The two boys would rush out of the car and sprint to the crystal clear waters of Cuba, an island that Christopher Columbus loved; he called it the "Pearl of the Antilles"* [a group of islands in the Caribbean Sea]. The sand was so white, silky soft and the agua* [water] was so pristine that the boys saw their toes, the bottom of the sea, and even little colorful peces* [fish]! Papi and Tío would also come into the water and play with the boys. Then they would eat a "sandwich" of jamón y queso* [ham and cheese] on Cuban [Italian-type] bread de manteca [Bread made of lard] with mayonesa* [mayonnaise]. It was so good after swimming in nature's amazing pool. Yet after eating, Luisito could not enter the water for three hours! This was a strict rule of los Tíos Luis y [and] Teresa, as well as of many Cubans. One must digest the food or you may get a "calambre" * [cramp] and drown! La playa was another reason that el niño Miguelito loved his native island of Cuba so much. It was a true paradise.

Feliz Navidad

La Navidad*, Christmas

La Navidad was the most special, happy and exciting time of the year. Miguelito looked forward to La Noche Buena* *[Christmas Eve]* at la casa* *[home]* de Tía Ofelia and "El Día de los Reyes,"* *[The Three Wisemen]*, January 6, because he would receive so many toys from the "Three Wisemen". La Noche Buena, December 24, was a huge celebration because Tío Alfonso who was a Chef in the Bronx, NY, always sent a lot of money: $25. [Tíos Alfonso y Guilla lived in NY with la prima Cayuya, who was disabled.] Then Abuela* *[Grandma]* Catuca and Tía Ofelia would buy a whole cerdo* *[pig]*! They would start roasting the pig in the morning, and also cook plátanos fritos* *[fried bananas]*, yucca, a salad with avocados, and the famous Cuban "frijoles negros", black beans with white rice called "Moros y Cristianos"* *[Moors and Christians]*, and much more! Miguelito loved the skin of the pig, but he felt sorry for the poor animal with an apple in his mouth! The entire *familia** was there, maybe 50 personas* *[persons]*. They played Christmas music, and they sang and enjoyed the holiday. Feliz Navidad!* *[Merry Christmas]*. It was an amazing evening with much food, drink, singing, and most importantly—la familia cubana. Miguelito would have this fond memory in his heart for life. Would the day be so very, very special in America?

The Three Wisemen, January 6

Ironically, one Christmas things changed. When he was seven years old, Miguel was told that he was only allowed two toys, a new rule of the new government. Why, Mami?? Mami explained that this was the way things were and they could not change it. Some children were getting nothing. Were they bad? No. There was no money, no toys, no Three Wisemen. So Miguelito was confused—"los Tres Reyes Magos," The Three Wisemen ran out of toys? He sensed something was wrong. However, he requested a bicycle and a ball, like a basketball/soccer ball. Mami and Papi seemed worried about the Three Wisemen bringing a bike, but el niño* *[boy]* Miguelito really wanted a bike. Finally the long awaited day arrived, January 6, and the little Cuban boy got up like a cubano loco* *[crazy]* and rushed where he was used to finding the entire living room filled with little trucks, boats, baseball glove, and so much more. On this day he saw nothing! Nervous and teary-eyed, he looked at Mami, and she said, "Come with me, Mijo* *[Mi hijo-my son]*. The boy was so hurt, devastated, scared… as he left the home, he looked around—still no bike! But then he suddenly saw Papi coming down the hill from Tío Luis' house—*he had a bike in his hand! Oh my God!* The Three Wisemen had delivered the bike at Tíos Luis and Teresa's home? Like a wild cowboy, he jumped on the gorgeous bicicleta* *[bicycle]*. The boy rode the bike rapidly down the block and to the right to his school. Many cubanitos were looking and pointing at him in awe. Miguelito was so very, very happy! Yet the other boys seemed to have nothing. This again made him sad, surprised, puzzled. Mami had said that they were not bad, but times, things had changed. This left a sick feeling in Miguelito's stomach. Sí *[yes]*, things had really changed in Cuba.

An American Plane Takes Pictures

One night it seemed quiet as las Abuelas* [Grandmas] watched la televisión [TV] and Mami and Papi were talking to neighbors in the backyard. To their surprise, nearby hungry thieves were stealing chickens in the middle of the night, and the neighbors would run out of their homes very angry with rifles looking for the thieves, who sped away with las gallinas* [chickens] in a sack. Suddenly someone said, "Mira!"* [Look up there!] Miguelito heard loud noises. He jumped up on the kitchen sink and looked out the window up in the dark sky. A light would go off, like a camera flash. They said it was an American plane taking pictures of a Cuban Naval base. Yet the boy saw flashes of lights in a straight string of illuminated dots going upwards towards the plane. Mami again rushed into the home and took Miguelito into the bedroom under the bed. The boy heard the next day that those "bombas" [bombs] fired up in the air came back down and would land. Mami was so scared. It was a very frightening time for this little Cuban boy, and actually for all the children of Cuba.

We're leaving Cuba!

Tío* *[Uncle]* Luis met an ambassador from Morocco, Africa, and they made a deal. Tío Luis gave him gold jewelry from his jewelry store, and the ambassador got *la familia** visas, a special document needed to leave Cuba. "Our prayers have been answered," expressed Isela—Mami. Mami and Papi had mixed emotions--they were surprised, happy and yet sad. Miguelito didn't know how to feel. His parents wanted to leave Cuba and go to América, but the little boy, siete * *[7]* years old, didn't know how he could leave his beautiful island, familia and amigos* *[friends]*. He didn't even speak English. He heard it was even very cold in Nueva York* *[NY]*. It was a very bad, ill feeling in Miguelito's stomach and heart.

La Promesa* (The Promise)

Before they could leave Cuba, Mami said she had to fulfill a promise. "A promise to whom, Mami?" Mijo* *[Mi hijo, my son]*, a promise to "El Señor, Dios* *[Sir, God]*. Mami had promised God that if her child were born healthy she would promise to do something special to express her gratitude to God. Miguelito did not know exactly what it was…One day Mami, el niño**[the boy]* and Abuela**[Grandma]* Catuca took a train to Oriente, several hours away. The train was exciting and fun for the little boy. When they arrived, they searched for a hotel, but the taxista* *[cab driver]* told Mami that the very few hotels were taken, so he offered his home. Mami would pay him something for the stay. Miguelito was so hungry, and the cab driver's wife made them a sánwich* *[sandwich]* of *"ropa vieja"** *["old clothes"]*, shredded beef with tomato sauce, which he ate with café con leche* *[coffee with milk]*. It was so, so delicious! Then they finally set out. The man drove them to a huge, bella* *[beautiful]* catedral* *[cathedral]*. There Mami and Abuela seemed very serious. The boy looked up many, many steps leading up to the giant, dark wooden doors. Suddenly Mami, who had a veil on her head, like Abuela, looked directly at the cross on top of the center of the church. She stared closely at the cross, as if hypnotized by Jesús on the crucifix. Mami then approached the left side of the bottom of stairs and respectfully knelt down on the first step. To Miguelito's surprise, she started to go up the stairs on her knees! The stairs had dirt and some pebbles on them, as Abuela Catuca attempted to clean them with a handkerchief—"No! Mama," expressed Mami to Abuela. This was part of "la promesa". Miguelito felt so bad for his Mami. Many people looked, respectfully, and would whisper to each other, "Una promesa". As she continued to look so seriously, directly at the crucifix, the devoted Cuban Mom finally reached the top, without ever stopping for a break. La Madre *[Mom]* then embraced her son and her mother. Isela had fulfilled her promesa. Miguelito felt so loved by his mamá. They may now leave for America!

Leaving la Patria* [Mother country] Cuba

Now Miguelito's familia* prepared to leave Cuba. Abuela* [Grandma] Catuca sewed Miguel a coat from a thick blanket. Abuela used her Singer sewing machine, as she looked through her old glasses, to make him a warm coat. Tío* [Uncle] Fernando wanted to create secret codes with Papi. This way they could write in codes and no one would know what they were saying. The little boy thought that all of this was mysterious and adventurous like a spy movie that he watched on his black and white TV with Papi. Their nice blue car would not go to Abuela* or the familia—they had to leave it for the Cuban government, although many in the familia needed a car. They gave away much clothing that would not fit in three suitcases. All of their belongings, Miguel's books, toys, and clothing would have to fit in one suitcase! Miguelito cried because his beloved bicycle, toys and books would have to stay, as they just didn't fit. Mami's jewelry would have to stay, given to relatives. This was not fair! Miguelito complained. Yet Mami explained to el niño [boy]—this was the high price of la libertad* precious *freedom*—America.

Saying Adiós [Goodbye] to la Familia-- The Last Day in Cuba

El niño [boy] could not imagine leaving beautiful Cuba, but the day had finally come. Mami had packed the three suitcases, which they had borrowed from la familia. Tíos Luis and Teresa came to pick them up. They kissed and hugged Abuela* María and Bisabuela* Amparo. Mami and las Abuelas cried much, but Papi and Miguelito did not, as the little boy was so frightened that he did not know how to express his feelings, but he knew that this was very serious. The dog Oso* [bear] seemed sad; he went into *Abuela** Amparo's room and hid under the bed. The other dog, Mochito, was sad and upset, so he barked loud at Papi, who touched his head with his infinite affection for "animales". Abuela Amparo, an often angry Spaniard, held up her cane and said, "Silencio, cállate!"* [shut up]. Mochito then put his head down in fear, but he still barked in sadness. Papi and son hugged Mochito, said adiós [Goodbye]. Papi so loved all animals as if they were family members.

Tío Luis drove to la casa* [home] of Tía Ofelia. There the whole familia was waiting in front of the home, even Sultán, the big German Sheppard. Miguelito saw everyone hugging Mami, Papi and him. Many of la familia* cried aloud, shedding great tears for them, as they would miss them very much. At some point Miguelito did not hear anything because it was like a bad dream. It was as if it were a sad movie and the sound was lost…He could not really believe it. Was this really happening to him? Mami and her sisters embraced, Tías Ofelia and Tía Lidia, and they did not want to let go, like glued together. Abuela Catuca hugged Mami, and gave her some words of encouragement to make them feel better. Abuela Catuca told Mami not to worry—this is what we had prayed for—America! (Yet she really didn't know that.) She would pray every night, like Abuela María, that the long boat ride to Africa would be safe. The neighbors came over to also bid farewell. Juan in the wheel chair and Titi, "el Negrito"* an African-American dear friend who always pushed Juan in the chair, also hugged the three. The big Sheppard Sultán wanted to desperately jump the fence to be with Papi, but the father went to him and gave him a giant hug, adiós-- goodbye. Sultán felt better, but not el niño Miguelito. Tío Luis said that they really had to go, as they had a long ride to Camaguey where the big cargo boat was waiting. They got into Tío's red and white car and left. In the back seat, Mami still cried in Papi's arms. He consoled her with affection. Miguelito was quiet, very, very scared; however, he didn't want to cry because that would upset Mami even more, so he kept it all in. Nervous and speechless, el niño did not utter a word.

"El bote grande."* *The big boat*

The boat seemed very large. It was a cargo boat because it transported sugar from Cuba to Morocco, a country in north Africa. Miguelito asked Papi whether they would see leones* and tigres*, [*lions and tigers*], but Papi laughed and said, no, that Casa Blanca, the city would not have a jungle and these animales*. However, Miguelito had no idea what to expect. Yet he knew that Mami and Papi were making the right decision for him and la familia*

Finally Tíos* [*Uncle and Aunt*] Luis y* and Teresa drove them to the boat. It was time to go on the big boat. It was so frightening for Miguelito to walk up that wood ramp while Mami held his arm so very firmly so he would not fall in the water. When they got on the boat, these soldiers welcomed them. The familia* had to show the visas. El niño* was still scared—would they get in trouble? Would they be allowed to leave? Would they get in trouble and go to jail like others? To their surprise, the Cuban soldiers were actually nice. They felt bad for la familia* leaving la patria,* [*their mother country*]. Papi asked them whether they were allowed any jewelry. The Cuban soldier said they could take any jewels they had---it was their property. At that point, Tío* Luis started putting earrings on Mami and giving them jewels to take out of the country. Miguelito did not realize that this gold jewelry would be money much needed for la familia in Africa and during the long journey to America and freedom.

the Boat Ride

As the big boat left Cuba, Miguelito was very sad. They were actually leaving the isla* *[island]* he so loved and was accustomed to for eight years of his happy life with los padres* *[parents]*, la familia*, los amigos* *[friends]*, especially Lilianita! He would miss his beautiful bici* *[bicycle]*, his libros* *[books]*, toys, los perros* *[dogs]* and even los pollos y el gallo bravo *[chickens and one angry rooster]*. Mostly he would miss la familia and los primos* *[cousins]* Conchita, Ginita, Aselita, Luisito and many others.

Miguelito met a very nice, lovely girl, Cristina and her madre* *[Mom]* on the boat. They were also leaving Cuba with a visa so they were leaving "legally," el niño* would hear. Those escaping if caught were thrown in prison for a very long time, others the little boy heard, disappeared escaping Cuba to Key West, in "la Florida" *[Florida]*. These stories made the little cubanito *[little Cuban]* very nervous; he had butterflies in his stomach for many years to come. Often he could not sleep worrying about leaving his country for another one which seemed very far away.

The little room of la familia had a crib for Miguelito, who was too big for it, so he slept in a fetal, bebé *[baby]* position, and Mami y* *[and]* Papi slept in bunk beds, like the sailors; Papi on the top bunk bead, Mami on the bottom. There was no bathroom in the tiny room, so they had to go out to one in the hallway, sometimes in the very cold, windy evening. El niño* asked Mami whether he can do "pi-pi" *[urinate]* in the sink, but Mami said, "No mijo." *[No son]*. Lo siento *[sorry]*. They ate with the Capitán* *[Captain]*, Cristinita *[little Cristina]*, her Mamá*, and the officers. The food was new and strange. For lunch they served a new meat called salami. He hated it, but Cristina ate it all. They also served a salad that he would eat a little of, and often served "cuscus"* which he also could not stand. So he often would hide the food in the cloth napkins, even in his pockets. Mami* would tell him, "Niño Come!"* *[Little boy--Eat!]*, but he just missed his Cuban comida* *[food]* so, so much! Snack time was tea and crackers. Tea?? Who drank tea?? Why not café con leche?* *[coffee with boiled milk]*. He did eat the crackers; they were eatable, not bad. For anything bad, there was always something good. It must be the prayers of Abuela María and those of la familia.

Playing on the boat with Cristina

Miguelito and Cristina played all day long. She actually spoke French. Her Mamá* knew French and made Cristina study it. Miguel and los padres* thought that was wonderful. Los niños *[the children]* played "el escondido"* *[hide and seek]* and other games. El cubanito* had one toy with him—a plastic, black gun. He and his amigos* *[friends]* used to play cowboys and Indians, or "Guerra"* *[war]*, and they all had toy guns, rifles and little green plastic soldiers in those days. Once Miguel shot an "enemy" soldier, his amigo* would be out of that battle. Now he and Cristina would fight evil spies and fictitious-make believe "bad guys" on the boat. Sometimes as Miguel and Cristina would walk the narrow hallways of the boat, a sailor would suddenly enter the hallway, so Miguel would quickly pull out his gun and shoot the sailor, who would actually fall to the ground. Playing dead-- "Está muerto!"* *[He's dead!]* Miguel would tell his female companion, as he blew the smoke from the barrel of his toy gun. Cristina would laugh, her bella* *[beautiful]* smile, and they would run off leaving the sailor "playing dead" on the ground.

"Gracias a Dios,"* *[Thank God]* Miguel had Cristinita to play with. Her Mamá* had become very good amiga* with the Capitán*, and would spend a lot of time with him. He had a nice big room with a desk. One time Papi* saw a bunch of crumpled papers in this garbage, so Papi, who had no paper to write letters to Cuba or Nueva York* [NY], went into his garbage to take some crumpled paper, but the Capitán* said no, por favor* *[please]*, have some fresh, new sheets. Then he gave Papi* a small stack of paper, "Muchas Gracias!"* *[Thanks a lot!]* said Papi and Mami with a big smile of gratitude. They seemed grateful for every little thing the familia* received on the boat. This would be a "life lesson" for the little, Cuban boy—always be grateful for everything in life—take nothing for granted, and always say por favor* *[please]* and gracias,* *[thanks]*, and thank God for all that we have.

Miguelito is missing!

One day the boat was very shaky, as the seas were rough, and very wavy. The boat now seemed not so big, as the overwhelming, angry ocean seemed to engulf and throw around the vessel like one of Cristina's rag dolls. On that dangerous day, Mami and Papi could not find the little boy. Even Cristina was worried and searching for that cubanito* running around the boat like Speedy Gonzalez*. Mami started to cry and Papi had that very nervous, scared look on his face, like the time the boy had crashed his bici* into the wall and his lips were bleeding. "Dónde está mi niño!"* *[Where is my boy??]*

El niño* Miguel was running around the boat as he often did, expressing his great energy in a confined space—el bote* *[boat]* He had noticed how the boat rocked back and forth like a bebe's* *[baby's]* cradle, but he was often playing his fantasy of spies— he and Cristina were the good guys. As he ran down the outside corridor of the boat, suddenly a huge, terrible wave smacked the boat the left—the little boy was thrown like a small toy and he was headed right for one of those port holes on the sides of the ship. Los padres* *[parents]* had warned him many times that he could fall right out into the careless, mean ocean which would swallow him like a small fish. However, Miguel instinctively outstretched his arms to the left and the right as if to hug someone; the force threw him so that his head went through the porthole—for a second he stared at the terrible ocean—the face of death--yet his outstretched arms actually saved his life. The cubanito had embraced la vida* *[life]*. The niño* turned sickly, pale white, as he pulled himself back to stand up on the deck. He had immediately thought of Mami's maternal advice, and then Papi. What would they think if he had fallen through that port hole? He now hugged the wall of the boat, terrified that these dangerous waters would again attack the boat.

The young Cubanito now embraced precious life. He escaped into the first door he could find and tried to traverse the boat through the narrow hallways. He ended up on the control tower learning instruments, trying to hold in his emtions and tears. Suddenly he saw Mami crying hysterically—"Dónde estabas?!!*" *[Where were you?]*. She hugged el niño* with a tremendous bear hug. Somehow, Mami's maternal instinct knew that her little hijo* *[son]* was in serious danger; "Gracias a Dios"* *[thank God]* he was ok. Miguelito would not dare tell his padres* what happened. In fact, he would not tell them for the next 20 years.

The exotic, frightening city of Casablanca, Morocco

La familia* Ruiz finally arrived safely to North Africa—Casablanca, Morocco. Miguelito el cubanito* had travelled across the Atlantic Ocean to Morocco, although his native Cuba was just 90 miles away from the greatest country on earth—America. Miguelito would miss Cristina, as she would be leaving with her madre* to France and then to the US. They looked at each other with very sad eyes, hugged, and she left with her mother. Unfortunately, they would never meet again. Forty years later, the boy would still miss her, his soul mate during the most difficult time in his life.

The little eight year old boy saw things he had never ever seen before. Women with their faces covered. Men with strange clothing, beards and very serious looks on their faces. Some of them would squat at the curb and urinate. This was shocking to la familia*. Beggars on every corner, as women begged in three or four languages. "Le ruego mi hijo tiene el brazo roto."* *[I beg you sir, my son has a broken arm.]* Yet the sailors warned them that the child's arm was not really broken. They would say this for money. Papi* would give them change, but Mami* got angry because la familia* needed money to get to Nueva York* *[NY]* Miguel felt so sorry for the Moroccan kids begging with their Mami. One time he looked through a basement window and saw three women sitting in a room with a rug, a table, four chairs, and a toilet. Papi explained that in Morocco men had more than one wife; it was allowed. "¿Por qué??" *[Why?]* asked el niño*. It was a very different cultura* *[culture]*

There were many scary stories. One blonde, German sailor was awaiting his beautiful fiancé, but as she traveled from Europe to Morocco, she disappeared. Miguel heard that she was kidnapped because she looked so different from them, blonde with blue eyes, attractive. The sailor showed everyone her picture. He was devastated. Miguel realized that this was real—not a spy movie.

How would they get to America from Africa?

Now la familia* Ruiz came to a very nervous time. The boat was leaving in a week. However, they needed to find a way to America, and get the money from la familia* to get to the US, and finally be approved by the American Consulate, the office which would allow their entering the US. Los padres* *[the parents]* decided that they would not go back on the boat to Cuba. They were determined to find a way to América, the land of freedom. Mami prayed to God every day.

After long days of worry and anxiety, and Papi sending telegrams to NY, thank God they found a boat going to NY; they got the money from la familia in the US., nonetheless, they had a very, very important meeting with the American Consul, the American man who had to approve their papers.

Miguelito was so nervous, as he felt the tension in Papi*, with that nervous look that strong Papi's* don't usually have, and poor Mami* wore her emotions on her sleeve, they would say; Isela was extremely apprehensive. They entered the office and shook hands with this big, rotund Americano* *[American]* The Americano* took out the folder and looked through the papers. He looked serious and maybe even angry? The tres* *[three]* Cubanos* *[Cubans]* were extremely apprehensive, anxious because the man did not speak for about a minute. The tall, fair man, wearing a white shirt, jacket and tie, as did Papi*, looked at Papi* and Mami* and said in English, "Your papers have not yet returned from Washington DC." Papi* looked panicked, turned very pale, wide eyed. Mami* sensed what was said. Mami* y Papi* held hands tightly. They looked at the large man in a sad desperation. All the way to Africa from Cuba in a long, dangerous trip and now what would they do in this very exotic country? "But, you know what," the Americano said. "You sure don't look like spies to me." Papi seemed suddenly hopeful. "So I'm going to approve your papers." Papi* and Mami* jumped up, Mami* screamed with tears of joy and jubilation; they hugged lovingly, hugged the Americano, told Miguelito to hug the man, so he sprinted to do so. They would be approved. Mami's prayers were answered again. El Americano* stamped their visas and they left very, very happily, as the three joined "manos" *[hands]*, in a ever so unique—loving, grateful union—la familia bella.* *[beautiful family]*

Going to the great America, a "Melting Pot" of Immigrants

La familia* Ruiz said adiós to el Capitán and the sailors, all of whom were very nice to them. In fact that last week they stayed on the boat, although they were not supposed to, because they could not afford a hotel.

They boarded another boat which ironically was filled with people who actually liked Communism, but had never lived it. The ride seemed much shorter and nicer. They had a room, and Miguelito had a small bed instead of a crib. Before he knew it, the morning came that the boat entered NY Harbor—the door to freedom. All of a sudden, the cubanito* saw a huge, green statue, a woman holding up a torch. Mami* burst into tears of joy and was held by Papi*. "La Estatua de Libertad,"* *[the Statue of Liberty], an incredibly beautiful and unforgettable sight.* The boat landed; they went through immigration where some people were detained, held and not allowed to enter América. Yet they were indeed allowed to enter Freedom. Papi,* Mami* and Miguelito, very tan because of weeks at sea, walked onto the streets of Nueva York* [NY]. Tíos* [Aunt and Uncle] Manolo and Rosa were not there because they did not have a car. Therefore, Papi* said, "Let's surprise them and take a cab," as Papi* had some dollars in his pocket. They entered a yellow NYC cab. The driver, to their pleasant surprise, spoke Spanish. He was very nice and welcoming. In fact he soon turned the meter off because he said the trip to Brooklyn would cost too much money. Miguelito saw a very different place with many tall, attached buildings and signs with foreign words. They arrived to Brooklyn, said "gracias"* to the cabby, and surprised Tío* Manolo when they knocked on his door. Los tíos* and primos* [cousins] Manny and Roger, embraced la familia*, and they shed more tears of joy. After an extremely long and adventurous journey, Miguelito had finally made it to freedom—Los Estados Unidos de America!* [USA!]

Edwards Brothers Malloy
Thorofare, NJ USA
March 22, 2016